Class Pets

More
Super ♡ Duper ♡ Royal ♡ Deluxe
books!

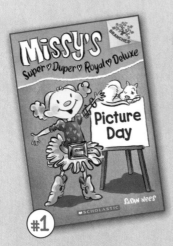

#1

#2

#3

#4

Missy's

Super ♡ Duper ♡ Royal ♡ Deluxe

Class Pets

By
SUSAN NEES

BRANCHES

SCHOLASTIC INC.

For Maggie and her bright little Stars

Library of Congress Cataloging-in-Publication Data

Nees, Susan.
Class pets   by Susan Nees.
p. cm. -- (Missy's super duper royal deluxe ; 2)
Summary: Missy wants to take home the class pets, but another girl, Tiffany, has already asked their teacher so Missy and her friend Oscar need to come up with a plan to make Tiffany change her mind.
ISBN 978-0-545-43852-0 (pbk.) -- ISBN 978-0-545-49610-0 (hardback) -- ISBN 978-0-545-54010-0 (ebook) 1. Rats as pets--Juvenile fiction. 2.Elementary schools--Juvenile fiction. [1. Rats--Fiction. 2. Elementary schools--Fiction. 3. Schools--Fiction.] I. Title.
PZ7.N384Cl 2013
813.54--dc23

                              2012035572

ISBN 978-0-545-49610-0 (hardcover) / ISBN 978-0-545-43852-0 (paperback)

Copyright © 2013 by Susan Nees

All rights reserved. Published by Scholastic Inc.
SCHOLASTIC, BRANCHES, and associated logos are trademarks and/or registered trademarks of Scholastic Inc.

12 11 10 9 8 7 6 5 4 3 2 1   13 14 15 16 17 18/0

Printed in China   38
First Scholastic printing, June 2013

Table of Contents

This is Melissa Abigail Rose.

But everyone calls her "Missy."

This is Missy's cat Pink.

Everyone calls him "Pink."

Mornings are always busy for Missy. But today was extra busy. Today was special. Today Missy was going to bring home a class pet. Missy had to get everything ready. She made a sign.

She packed her lunch box.

...pudding for me, lettuce for Rambo the snake, gummy bears for Eenie-Meenie, Miney, and Moe...

She helped Pink get dressed.

Hold still, Pink. We need to look our very best today.

And most important of all, Missy fixed up
her room. Her room needed to be ready.
Ready for pets! Ready for fun! Ready for
ACTION! Missy searched high and low,
looking for what she would need.

On her shelves, she found a bottle of
jumbo bubbles, an alarm clock, three
rubber fish, one roller skate, and a map
of Walla Walla, Washington.

Under her bed, she found a race car, a train set, a camera, a hula hoop, and an accordion.

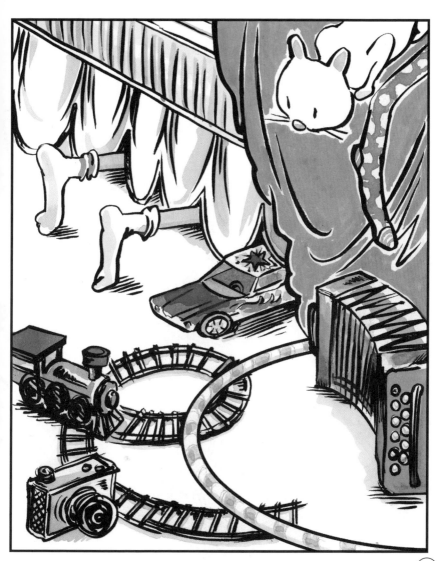

In her closet,
she found...

an
umbrella,

a roll
of tape,

a tea set,

spy
glasses,

and a
flashlight.

Now everything was ready. Well, not quite everything. There was just one teeny-tiny thing left to do.

Missy had to ask her mother....

But Missy's mother said that the class pets would be noisy. And messy. And smelly.

And she said:

What if they were to get loose?

Missy's mother said NO. But Missy was not about to give up that easily.

Missy tried asking
sweetly...

Pretty please
with sugar
on top?

Plllleeeeaasssseee?

slowly...

PLEASE!

loudly...

Please?!

Uh-oh.

She even tried
standing on her head.

13

But still Missy's mother said no.

This time, Missy's mother did not say no.

Chapter Two
Noodlehead

When Missy got to school, she was super duper excited to share her news.

At the end of the day, I get to choose a class pet to bring home. And I am going to choose Eenie-Meenie, Miney, and Moe. We are going to have a fashion show and a circus and a parade and a rodeo and . . .

But before Missy could finish,
in walked trouble. Big trouble.
It was Tiffany. Tiffany was the
new girl. Tiffany was big. Tiffany
was loud. Tiffany had hairy arms.
But worst of all, Tiffany was mean.

Chapter Three
Oscar's Note

Now remember Missy:

no name-calling,
no nay-saying,
no flim-flamming,
no gum-chewing,
blah, blah, blah...

Missy's teacher, Miss Snodgrass, was a real stickler when it came to rules.

When class started, it was hard for Missy to concentrate.

Missy tried to listen. She really did.
But it was no use.

Rambo the snake
in a fashion show?
No way.

Mozart the goldfish
in a circus?
No!

**Snickers the turtle in a parade?
Forget it!**

**George Washington the bird
in a rodeo?
Nope! Not happening!**

Missy decided one thing was for sure—
she was going to need a plan.

She knew just who could help: Oscar.
Oscar was a thinker. Oscar would know
what to do.

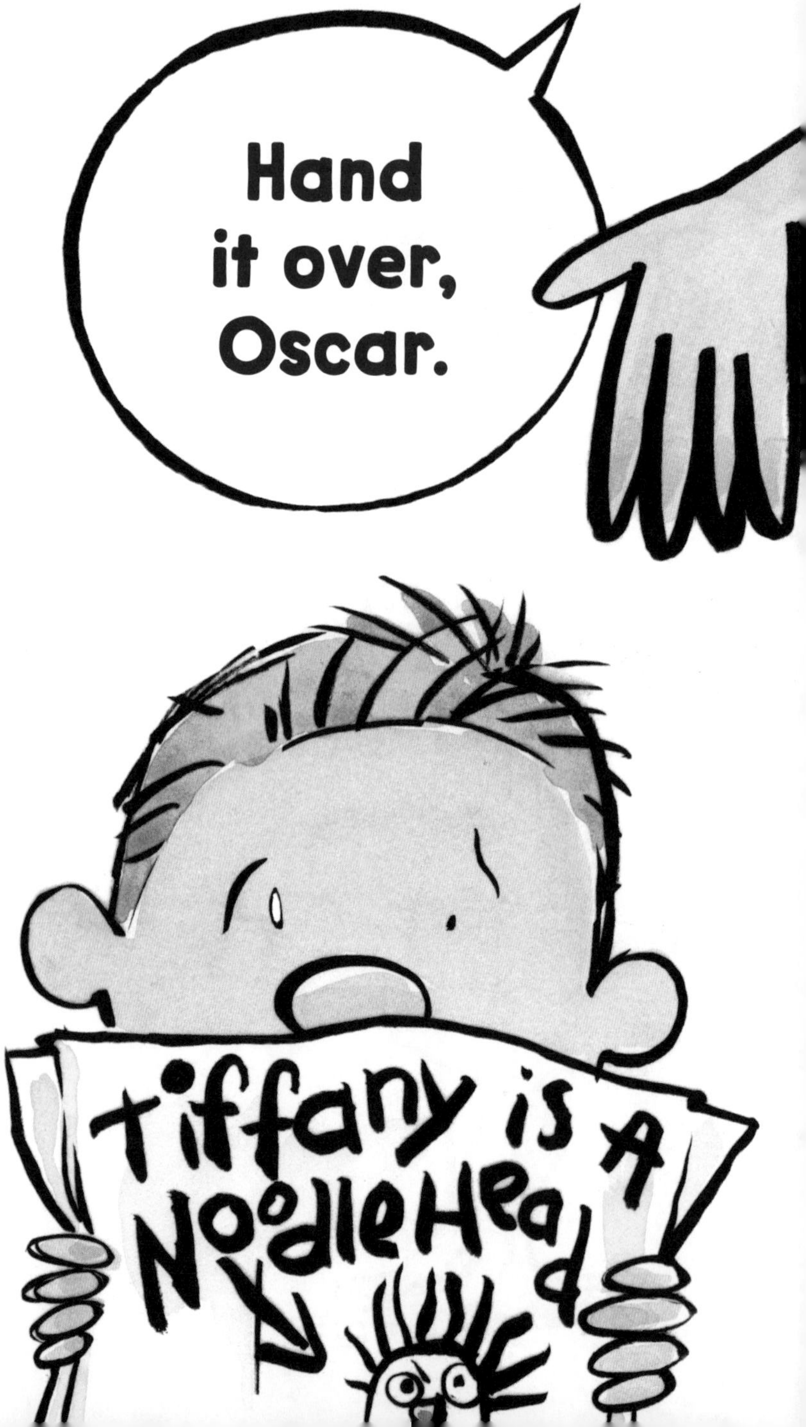
Hand it over, Oscar.
Tiffany is A NoodleHead

Chapter Four
Green Gummy Bears

Oscar, I'm surprised at you! You know our rules.

Now, line up quietly, everyone.

When I am talking: eyes looking, ears listening, and absolutely no monkey business!

It's library time.

Missy was glad when it was time to go to the library. Missy liked the library.

It was a good place to think.

Hi, Oscar. What are you reading?

Shhh.

But Oscar was no longer listening to Missy. Oscar was too busy thinking about facts.

Chapter Five
The Secret Plan

TICK...

TOCK...

TICK...

TOCK...

SIGH!

Missy could not wait for recess.
It seemed to take forever for the
bell to ring.

On the playground, Missy put her plan into action.

You can't catch me.

Yoo-hoo!

Tiffany! I have a secret.

Miss Mary Mack Mack Mack,

What do you want to do?

I don't know. What do you want to do?

Let's chase boys.

Chapter Six
Pet Parade

At the end of the day, Missy knew what was coming. And she didn't like it one bit.

Tiffany chose Eenie-Meenie, Miney, and Moe.
Taylor chose George Washington the bird.

The twins chose Snickers the turtle. Then
Paulette chose Rambo the snake.

And Missy got Mozart—the goldfish.

Hah!

Rats ran. Students screamed. Books flew and desks toppled. But that didn't stop Missy.

65

Missy knew just how to find
Eenie-Meenie, Miney, and Moe.

Miss Snodgrass said Missy was a hero.
Miss Snodgrass said Missy could take
home any class pet she wanted. When
Missy chose Eenie-Meenie, Miney, and
Moe, no one was surprised.

And it was.

The End

Susan Nees

grew up on a farm, so she always had plenty of animals to play with. One hot summer day, Susan and her sister dressed up baby pigs in doll clothes and rigged up a blanket over the clothesline to serve as their "hospital." The sisters fed their "patients" green garden pea "pills." This went on until the piglets broke free, running across the yard trailing socks and bonnets. Today, Susan lives in Georgia with her family, Jodo the dog, and a small flock of chickens. Missy's Super Duper Royal Deluxe is Susan's first children's book series.